SNOOPING CAN BE

Un-Merry

Books by Linda Hudson Hoagland
from Jan-Carol Publishing, Inc:

LINDSAY HARRIS MURDER MYSTERY SERIES:
SNOOPING CAN BE DANGEROUS
SNOOPING CAN BE CONTAGIOUS
SNOOPING CAN BE DEVIOUS
SNOOPING CAN BE DOGGONE DEADLY
SNOOPING CAN BE HELPFUL–SOMETIMES
SNOOPING CAN BE UNCOMFORTABLE
SNOOPING CAN BE SCARY
SNOOPING CAN BE REGRETTABLE
SNOOPING CAN BE UN-MERRY

THE BEST DARN SECRET
ONWARD & UPWARD
MISSING SAMMY

SNOOPING CAN BE
Un-Merry

LINDA HUDSON HOAGLAND

Jan-Carol
Publishing, Inc
"every story needs a book"

Snooping Can Be Un-Merry
Linda Hudson Hoagland

Published September 2024
Little Creek Books
Imprint of Jan-Carol Publishing, Inc.
All rights reserved
Copyright © 2024 by Linda Hudson Hoagland
Front Cover and Book Design: Tara Sizemore

ISBN: 978-1-962561-43-3
Library of Congress Control Number: On file

You may contact the publisher:
Jan-Carol Publishing, Inc.
PO Box 701
Johnson City, TN 37605
publisher@jancarolpublishing.com
www.jancarolpublishing.com

This book is dedicated to my sons,
Michael E. Hudson and
Matthew A. Hudson

DEAR READER

Lindsay Harris and family are at it again as they snoop into the person or persons who killed a neighbor, Otis Greene.

Lindsay wants her children to snoop from a distance, but that doesn't happen when each of them are taken away by persons unknown to places unknown.

The snow creates a problem for Jed, her newspaper reporter friend, and herself as they search frantically to find her children.

Follow Lindsay and Jed as they try to discover the truth about the death of Otis Greene and find her children so they can celebrate Christmas.

This is the ninth volume of the *A Lindsay Harris Murder Mystery* series, and it takes on the search for the truth about Otis Greene and the return of Lindsay's children.

Lindsay struggles to make sure that Christmas for her family is not destroyed by the idea that *Snoopng Can Be Un-Merry.*

Chapter 1

"Mom, there is a policeman at the door!" shouted Ryan. I dropped the sheet onto the unmade bed and headed to the living room.

"Ask him to come in, Ryan," I said loudly.

"There are three of them, Mom."

"Okay, ask them to come on into the living room," I told him impatiently.

As they trooped into my living room, I felt the feeling of dread envelope me. I didn't recognize any of them.

"Are you Lindsay Harris?" asked the man in the business suit. The other men were in uniforms.

"Yes, I am. Who are you?"

"I'm Detective William and with me is Detective Martin. We are investigating the death of your neighbor, Otis Greene," he said in his professional voice.

"I heard that he had passed away, but I didn't realize it wasn't from old age or genuine cussedness," I said venomously.

"I understand you and Mr. Greene had a disagreement recently. Would you tell me what that was about and why it became violent?" asked Detective Williams.

1

"First of all, who told you about the argument?" I demanded.

"I can't disclose that information, but I need to know all about your disagreement with Mr. Greene," said the detective.

"Did you ever meet Mr. Greene?" I asked the detective.

"No, I did not have the pleasure," he said.

"Pleasure is not the word to describe meeting him," I snapped.

"Okay, Ms. Harris, why do you say that?" asked the detective in a stern tone.

"Otis Greene never met a person he liked. No matter how hard you would try to befriend him, he would run you off like you were his worst enemy. He especially hated my children."

"What was your most recent run-in with him about?" asked the detective.

"My son, Ryan, and a couple of his friends were playing football," I said. "The football was kicked into his yard accidentally, and he wouldn't let Ryan get it. Ryan came into the house to get me, and I went out to ask him to return the football.

"Well...he got in my face and said he was not returning the football. If it was in his yard, it belonged to him. I called him a crazy old coot, and I told him I wanted the football back. He picked the football up and threw it at me with all of his might. I tore off after him to punch him out if I could get close enough."

"What happened next?" asked Detective Williams.

"Nothing. I couldn't catch up to him, so I turned around and went home. That's the last time I saw him."

"What about your son? What did he do?"

"He was already in the house. Do you really think an eleven-year-old boy would kill Otis Greene?" I asked.

"No, not really, but we have to check on anyone who has

had any kind of conflict with Otis Greene," said the detective. "Do you have any more children?"

"Yes, sir, I have twin daughters who are fourteen."

"Do you think they would know anything about the death of Otis Greene?"

"No, if they knew anything, they would have told me. I'm sure of that."

"Where are they?"

"Visiting a friend down the street. They will be home before dark."

"It's almost dark now," said the detective.

"They'll be here," I said.

The door burst open, and in walked Emily and Ellen. Both of them were giggling and pushing on each other. They were shaking off the snow and cold while removing their coats. When they spotted the strangers sitting in the living room, they halted the silliness immediately.

"Emily, Ellen, this is Detective Williams, and he wants to talk to you about Mr. Greene," I said warily. I wasn't sure how the girls would feel about talking to legal strangers.

"Who killed him?" asked Emily.

"That's what they are trying to find out," I explained.

"Ms. Harris, is there another room where I can talk with Emily with only you and Emily present?" asked Detective Williams.

"Okay, yes, you can use my bedroom. It's at the end of the hall on the right," I said as I started walking, followed by Emily and the detective.

I wasn't comfortable with this, but I didn't think there was anything I could do about it. One way or another, the detective or his partner would find a way to talk with them.

"Mom, what am I supposed to say?" whispered Emily.

"The truth," I whispered in response.

I sat on the bed next to Emily and steered Detective Williams to the side chair.

"Young lady, what is your name?" he asked.

"Emily Harris."

"How long have you known Otis Greene?"

"Ever since he moved into the house next door. Mom, how long ago did that happen?" asked Emily.

"I guess it has been around three years," I answered Emily.

"Have you had any problems with him?" asked Detective Williams.

"Yes," she answered warily.

"What kind of problems?" he continued.

"He is just mean and hateful about everything. I tried to stay away from him when he was alive. I have no idea who killed him, but most people who knew him won't be missing him at all," said Emily truthfully.

"Well, I think you answered any questions I was going to ask with that statement. I will speak with the other young lady now."

Emily left the room and Ellen walked in to face the questioning.

"What is your name?" he asked gruffly.

"Ellen Harris," she answered cheerfully.

"You seem to be a happy young lady," said the detective.

"I am, sir, but I put on a front when I'm nervous," Ellen explained.

"Why are you nervous?"

"Because Mr. Greene died and you think he was killed," she said as a frown formed on her lips. "I didn't do it. I hope you know that."

"I don't think you or your sister killed him. I was just hoping you might have seen something or maybe heard something that I could check out."

"I'm sorry, but I haven't heard a thing. I will let you know if I hear anything about who killed him. He really wasn't a very nice man, so I'm sure others might want him dead."

"Thank you," said Detective Williams.

The three legal persons exited my life for the moment. I just knew, deep down in my heart, that they would be back.

Chapter 2

"Mom, what should we do about Mr. Greene?" asked Emily.

"What do you mean?" I asked warily.

"Shouldn't we do some snooping to find out what happened?" Emily answered with another question.

"That might be dangerous," I said softly. "It's almost Christmas, and I don't think we should get into that right now."

"That didn't stop us before now. Anyway, he was so hateful I don't think anyone would care if he's dead. We need to do what his family should be doing, if he has any family."

I was so proud of Emily for even caring about what happened to Otis Greene. But I was afraid of sticking my nose into a situation about which I knew nothing. We have done just that before; so, I guess she was bound and determined that we should do it again. Emily was too much like me.

Just how we were going to find out who separated Otis Greene from his life was going to be a real challenge. I didn't know him well at all, and I was sure the girls didn't know him well. Trying to figure out where to start was definitely a problem, but we were going to do it regardless of whether it was Christmas or not.

6

I gathered my brood together for a family conference. My brood consisted of Emily and Ellen, my twin fourteen-year-old daughters, and Ryan, my son at age eleven. We weren't an especially strong force, but when we got started, we were usually successful in finding the hidden truth.

"Guys, Emily thinks we need to find out who killed Otis Greene. What do you think about doing that?" I asked in a soft tone. I didn't want to force them into a decision with which they didn't agree.

Motherhood can sometimes be a balancing act, and this was one of those times.

"We really need to find out, because the police don't seem to be too interested," said Emily as she tried to persuade us to jump into snooping mode.

"Why should we care? He was such a mean man," said Ryan.

"He might have had a reason to be so mean," said Emily in response.

"What do you think about this, Ellen?" I asked.

"I never liked him, not one little bit. He cussed at me, and he tried to put his hands in places he shouldn't have touched, but he was alone. He had no friends that I ever saw. Maybe we should snoop into this," said Ellen as she forced a controlled tone.

"When did he put his hands on you?" I demanded. "Why didn't you tell me about that?"

"I didn't want you to get mad at me because I had been talking with him. Anyway, he's dead now, so he can't do it again," explained Ellen.

"If something like that happens to any of you, please tell me about it," I said.

All of them hung their heads and whispered, "Yes."

"Okay, now where do we start?" asked Emily.

"Is the crime scene tape still intact?" I asked.

"No, it looks like someone has torn it down," Ryan said. "It's just lying there on the ground, and the little bit of snow we had is covering it up."

"Have any of you seen anyone going in or out of the house?" I asked.

"No, just the police and the detectives," said Ellen.

"You guys have been keeping a close eye on the place, haven't you?" I asked accusingly.

"Well—yes," said Emily. "Whoever killed Otis Greene could come after us. He lives only a couple of houses away. It could happen."

"You're right about that, but I think it was someone who had a grudge against him. His cussedness probably got him killed," I said as I tried to discourage them from thinking they could be killed tomorrow or the next day.

"Let's hope so," commented Ellen.

Chapter 3

Our next step into the mystery concerning the death of Otis Greene was to be observation.

"Emily, Ellen, Ryan...I want you guys to take turns watching Mr. Greene's house from our house," I said. "Don't go any closer. Just watch to see if anyone goes in or out," I finished sternly so they would get the message to stay away from his house.

"What about his back door?" asked Emily. "If I wanted to sneak in, I would go around to the back of the house."

"Okay, one of you can sit on the front porch, and one of you should go out back in the backyard. How does that sound?" I asked.

"We can't do that every day. We have other things we have to do," said Ellen.

"I know, but whenever you can, just watch," I said. I was hoping they would keep their distance from the Greene house.

"I'll take the first watch from the front," said Emily as she grabbed her coat and gloves.

"I'll go to the back. How long should we stay?" Ryan asked.

"Until you get tired or you see someone. If you see someone, come and get me. I don't want either of you going over to that house without me."

I knew the kids would get bored with just sitting and watching, so I checked on them every few minutes to see if they were staying put and not walking to the Otis Greene house.

I was working around the interior of my house, dusting and vacuuming, and of course checking on Emily and Ryan. Ellen was in her room, so I didn't have to worry about her.

I glanced up from the floor and caught sight of Ryan walking passed the side window. I pecked on the pane of glass to get his attention, but he was gone out of my vision. I snapped the off button on the vacuum and made my way to the front of the house.

I jerked the door open and saw no one.

"Ryan, Emily, where are you?" I said loudly.

No answer.

"Emily, Ryan, answer me!" I screamed.

I could hear voices in the distance, but they sounded like they were coming from children playing in the snow, not Emily and Ryan.

"Ryan, Emily, where are you?" I mumbled as I walked toward the front door.

"Ellen," I said as I entered the house.

"What?"

"Let's lock the doors and go find Emily and Ryan," I said as I walked to the front door and snapped the lock. I grabbed my keys and Ellen was standing right next to me.

"What happened?" Ellen asked.

"I don't know, but I can't find either one of them. We need to go to the Greene house. That's probably where they were headed," I said as I went to the back door, snapped that lock, and ushered Ellen out the door with me.

Chapter 4

"Where are we going, Mom?" asked Ellen as she pulled her coat together to fight the cold air.

"I don't know just yet," I said. "Right now, we are going for a walk to look for Ryan and Emily." I tugged at my coat and shoved my hands deep into the pockets.

"Are we going to look around the Otis Greene house?" asked Ellen.

"Yes, it's on the way as we are walking," I answered.

I walked slowly, turning my head side to side, searching for a sign or a sound.

The closer we got to the Greene house, the more nervous I became.

"Mom, are you alright?" asked Ellen after she glanced at me and saw that I was visually shaking.

"Yes, yes, I'm fine. I'm just cold," I lied.

"Mom, I can see that you're not fine. You must know something that I don't know. Now, tell me why you are shaking."

"I'm worried, that's all. Two of my children are missing, and I don't know why they are gone." I tried to control the flood of tears that were building up behind my eyelids.

11

"We'll find them. I know we will, and they are going to have a lot of explaining to do," Ellen said as she tried to console me.

"Yes, they will surely have to talk a lot to get out of this mess," I said. "Stop, don't go any farther."

"Why? Did you hear something? I didn't see anything or anyone. Did you?"

"The crime scene tape is gone," I whispered excitedly. "There is a light on inside the house. See, it's over there. No—it moved. It must be a flashlight. It moved again. We need to get a little closer so we can look in a window."

"No, Mom, they might grab us, and then how would we be able to help Ryan and Emily?" said a cautious Ellen.

I looked at her and was amazed that she was being so safety conscious.

"Now you're acting like Emily. When did that happen?" I asked with a grin.

"Mom, stop it. You know it's a twin thing," Ellen replied.

"I want to get a little closer. Let me know if you see anyone coming. Okay, Ellen?"

Ellen didn't answer, but I knew she was paying attention.

I crossed the front yard and proceeded to the side yard where I had gotten a glimpse of the light that flashed in the window.

I was frightened about what I was doing and especially about what I might see, but I kept walking. I scrunched my body down as I moved along the side of the house so that anyone inside couldn't see me sneaking up to the window.

When I was directly underneath the windowsill, I rose up slowly to peer inside. Total darkness was all I could see.

I moved away from that window and followed the yard that

was slightly downhill to the next window. I stood on my tiptoes to peek inside and, again, saw only darkness.

I peered ahead to the back of the house, where I saw a small porch extending out a bit from the side of the structure.

I heard a shuffling sound, and I was afraid to go any farther into the unknown.

I moved as fast as I could to get back to the street where Ellen was waiting for me.

Ellen was no longer where I left her.

"Ellen?" I whispered loudly.

No answer. This no-answer business was getting old.

"Ellen, where are you?" I whispered harshly.

I looked up and down the street, but she was nowhere to be found. I could not see any of her tracks in the snow, because they were almost gone.

Chapter 5

"What is going on?" I screamed.

"You got a problem, lady?" asked an elderly man who appeared on the front porch of the house that was located next to the Greene house.

"Yes, yes, I do. Did you see what happened to the young girl that was standing here?" I sputtered.

"No, I didn't see no girl," he said in a weak voice. "I just came outside when I heard you scream. Who was the girl you're looking for, and why are you looking for her?"

"She's my daughter, and she was waiting for me to come back," I answered.

"Where did you go, and why did you leave her here alone?" he questioned me.

"I was looking for my other daughter, her twin, and my son, Ryan. Now all three of them are gone," I explained between sobs.

"Don't worry, lady," he said in a much softer tone. "They'll come back. Kids always return home."

"I don't think so, but I can hope," I said. "By the way, I'm Lindsay Harris. Who are you?"

14

"Marvin Mason. I have lived here all my life," he said.

"Do you know who lives in this house?" I asked.

"The man who used to live there was Otis Greene. I don't like to speak ill of the dead, but he wasn't a very nice person." He looked around to see if anyone was listening.

"That's what I heard. He was murdered, you know," I said as I tried to get more information from him about his neighbor.

"That's what the policeman told me when he asked me a lot of questions. I couldn't tell him much because I didn't associate with Greene too often. We nodded at each other and that was about it."

"Who are you afraid of, Mr. Mason?" I asked.

"What do you mean?" he asked.

"You're talking in a whisper, and you keep looking around to see if anyone is close enough to hear you talk. Who are you afraid might hear you talking with me?"

"Some of his friends might be around," he said. "They look like some really rough characters. I'm getting too old to be getting into any kind of a fight. I've got to go inside now. I'm cold, and it's not safe to be out here."

He turned around and walked to his front door, where he let himself inside, slammed the door, and extinguished the dim light.

That was when I noticed it was almost dark. Still no Ellen.

I walked back to the house, let myself inside, and sat on the sofa to cry. The tears had to come out, and they did just that.

When I was able to think again, I tried to decide what my next step would be. *Should I call 9-1-1 or just sit here and wait for a while? Maybe I should call Jed to see if he could give me a hand in deciding what to do.*

15

What I really wanted to do was go to the house where Otis Greene used to live and break down the door so I could get inside to look for my three children.

That wasn't going to happen, and I knew that.

I picked up the telephone and punched in Jed's number.

Chapter 6

Jed's telephone rang and rang, but I wasn't going to hang up. I needed somebody to talk with, and I wanted that somebody to be Jed. After about 20 rings, he answered.

"Hey, Lindsay, what's up?"

"I need your help," I said as, once again, I tried to control the mounting tears.

"What's wrong?" he asked.

"My kids," I sobbed, "are gone."

"Gone where?" he asked softly, trying not to upset me more than I already was.

"I don't know," I managed to get out before I gave way to the next wave of tears.

"Did they run away?" he asked.

"No, I think someone has taken them," I cried.

"Why? Where? Who would do that to you? Your ex-husband wouldn't have taken them, would he?"

I paused before answering, because that thought had not entered my head.

"No, I don't think so. I haven't heard from him in quite a while. He hasn't paid his child support, but I have arrived at the point that we can get by without it. I don't think he would want to get me angrier than I already am, but you never know. I'm not going to travel down that road until I have to."

"Who do you think took your kids?"

"Someone connected to the Otis Greene murder," I suggested.

"Who is or was Otis Greene?" he asked.

"A neighbor who wasn't liked by anyone, but he is dead, so it wasn't him. He had friends that would go in and out of his house, according to his neighbor, which looked a little rough. I think they might have taken the kids."

"Why?" Jed asked.

"Well, we were trying to watch the Greene place from our house from the front and back porches," I said. "Ellen was in her room, and I was vacuuming. I saw Ryan walk past the side window from the back to the front, and by the time I got to the front door, both he and Emily were gone."

"You said all three of them were gone. What happened to Ellen?"

"Ellen and I went for a walk, hoping to find Emily and Ryan. When we got to the Greene house, I decided to try to see in through a window to find a light I had spotted inside. While I walked down the side of the house to look inside two different windows, someone took Ellen, because when I went back to where she was waiting for me, she was gone."

"You didn't hear her scream? You didn't see anyone?" Jed asked.

"No and no, to both questions. I have no idea who took her or where they went."

"Did you call the police?"

"Not yet," I said.

"Are you going to call the police?" he asked.

"I guess so. I wasn't sure what I should do because I don't want whoever took them to do any harm to them."

"Go ahead and call them. I'll be on my way to help you look for them," he said excitedly.

"I don't want this in the newspaper, Jed," I said sternly.

I knew it was the kind of story he loved to write about, because he was a newspaper columnist.

"I will eventually write about it, but not until we find the kids and get them back to you safe and sound," Jed assured me.

"No, never," I sputtered. "They might have friends who will take care of business and kill all of us."

"All right, all right, but I will be there as soon as I can. In the meantime, call 9-1-1 and tell them everything you told me."

Chapter 7

I called 9-1-1, and a car was dispatched right away. The patrol car was followed by two detectives in a separate car.

The patrol officer took down the necessary information for the paperwork, then Detective Williams started to talk with me. I did my best not to cry, and for the most part, I was successful. I could tell from his tone of voice while questioning me that he thought I was making the whole story up and pulling it all from my imagination.

"Why are you asking me all of these stupid questions and not looking for my kids?" I demanded after the second hour of never-ending, repetitive questions.

Before the detective could answer my question, Jed walked into the house, escorted by the police officer who was stationed outside.

"You are?" asked the detective as he stared menacingly at Jed.

"I'm a friend of Lindsay and her kids. I'm going to help her find her missing children," Jed said without hesitation.

"Are you the father?"

"No, sir, I'm not," Jed answered. "Like I said, I'm a friend of Lindsay and her kids."

"I want your name, address, and telephone number, and then I'm going to ask you to leave," said the detective in a stern, professional tone.

"Lindsay, do you want me to leave?" asked Jed.

"No, please let him stay," I cried. "I need his help to get through this."

"Are you two a couple?" asked the detective.

"Not in the way you are implying," stated Jed just as professionally as the detective had been earlier. "We are friends and have been for several years. I will be staying here to help Lindsay."

"What do you do for a living? You look familiar to me."

"I'm Jed Thompson, and I work for the Bristol Newspaper."

"You're a reporter," said the detective. "You need to leave."

"I'm her friend, and that's why I'm staying," Jed replied harshly.

"Please let him stay," I pleaded.

"Sit down, Mr. Thompson. I need to ask you some questions since you won't leave."

"Fine, fire away," said Jed.

"What do you know about the disappearance of the three children?"

"Only what Lindsay told me on the telephone," Jed replied.

"And what was that?"

"That they had disappeared. Two were gone, and then the third one. That's when she asked me to help find them."

"The police have the descriptions, and they are looking for them as we speak. Where do you plan to look to find them?" asked the detective.

"Anywhere and everywhere, especially around this neighborhood," Jed said. "I don't think they have been taken very far. Someone would have seen them if they are alive."

"God! Don't tell me they might be dead!" I screamed.

"Lindsay, you know that's a possibility, but we are not going to believe that has happened," Jed said. "Do you understand?"

Chapter 8

"Do you know this Otis Greene who Ms. Harris has mentioned as having been murdered?" the detective asked Jed as he stared at him with a piercing look.

"No, never heard of him before today," Jed replied.

"Do you know anything about Otis Greene personally, Ms. Harris?"

"No, only that he lived a couple of houses over from us," I replied.

"Why do you think his death has anything to do with the disappearance of your children?"

"It's too much of a coincidence for me to think anything else."

"Why is that?"

"When the kids, Emily and Ryan, stationed themselves in the front and back of the house to watch the comings and goings of the Greene house, they suddenly disappeared. Wouldn't you think it was related?"

"Maybe, maybe not," said the detective. "As you said, it could be a coincidence."

"I thought you cops didn't believe in coincidence," interrupted Jed.

23

"We don't," said the detective.

"Can we stop all of this talking and look for my kids?" I asked in exasperation.

"I'm going to leave my card with you, Ms. Harris. If you remember anything new, call me at that number any time, day or night," said Detective Williams.

"That's it? That's all you can tell me?" I begged.

"For now, but I will get back to you as soon as possible. The officers are canvassing your neighborhood, asking questions. I will let you know if they find anything."

Detective Williams walked through the opened front door to leave.

I stood up for a moment as the detectives left the house, but I collapsed onto the sofa when I realized Williams was gone.

"What am I supposed to do now, Jed?" I asked sadly.

"We're going to go find the kids," he said. "Maybe we can figure out who killed Otis Greene while we're at it." Jed grabbed my hand and pulled me from the sofa.

I followed Jed, but I had little hope that we would find my children. All I could do was pray.

Chapter 9

When we walked out into the darkness, I noticed that my house was encircled with crime scene tape. The snow was beginning to fall again, reminding me of the season.

"Why did they put that tape out?" I asked Jed.

"They think there was a crime committed here," he answered.

"My kids were taken by someone else. I didn't do anything with them or to them," I sputtered.

"They don't know that until they go further into the investigation," he explained.

"This is a nightmare," I whispered.

"That it is," said Jed. "Keep your eyes open, Linds, you might see something important."

The streetlights were dim and getting dimmer because of the falling snow, but every little bit of illumination helped. There were some houses that were completely dark and a few that had a little bit of illumination that I assumed were night lights. Some had Christmas lights blazing in the darkness.

The Otis Greene house was totally dark when we passed

it the first time. On the return trip, I thought I saw a glimmer of light.

"Did you see that?" I asked Jed.

"I think so, but it went out really quick. I'll pull over a couple of houses up ahead so we can watch for it again. I don't think the cops are around here any longer. I don't see any of their cars."

We waited and watched until neither one of us could hold our heads up. I finally woke up as the daylight peeked through the windshield.

When I looked around, I saw someone running past the car.

"Jed, wake up. Somebody went running that way," I said as I pointed to the sidewalk in front of us.

Jed started the car and slowly pulled away from the curb.

"I don't see him. Where did he go?" he asked.

"Up ahead. I can just barely see him," I said with a flush of excitement racing through me.

"I still don't see him."

"Just keep driving straight ahead. I will keep an eye out for him."

Suddenly, he was gone.

"I lost him. He has totally disappeared from sight," I said solemnly.

"Did you get a look at him?" asked Jed.

"No, he was running too fast," I said.

"What was he wearing?"

"Jeans and a green jacket or coat. That's all I saw."

"I'll pull over again. Maybe he will come out of hiding if he thinks we are gone."

"This is hopeless," I said.

"Is that him?" asked Jed as he pointed to the area where I

had seen the man disappear.

"Yes, I think so."

"I'm after him," said Jed as he began following the mystery man again.

We finally ran him to ground, and we both jumped out of the car to confront him.

As mystery man laid on the cold, snowy ground struggling to regain control of his breathing, both of us stood over him and glared. From the way he was acting, we could tell he was afraid of moving away from us.

"Why were you running?" Jed screamed at the man.

At first, the mystery man wouldn't answer Jed's question. When Jed asked him again, using his toe directed at mystery man's ribs, there was an answer.

"I didn't want to see what was going to happen to those kids," he whispered.

"What kids?" Jed asked.

"Her kids," he said and pointed at me.

"Lindsay, do you know this guy?" Jed asked me.

"No, I've never seen him before. What were they going to do to my kids?" I asked the mystery man as I tried to keep myself from kicking him. "Why were they doing anything to my kids? Who is doing it?"

"I can't tell you. He will kill me," sputtered the mystery man.

"If he doesn't kill you, I will," I said as I directed a quick kick into his ribs.

"Lindsay, stop it," Jed said. "We will get him up and call the detective to come and get him. In the meantime, we need to tie him up and put him in the trunk of my car. Here are the keys... Go get the rope out of my trunk, and we can get out of here."

Chapter 10

"Detective Williams."

"This is Lindsay Harris, Detective," I began. "We have a man in our possession who knows where to find my kids. He's not willing to tell me where they are, so I thought you might get the information out of him."

"Where is this guy right now?" Williams demanded.

"Locked in the trunk of Jed's car, so you need to hurry," I said as I disconnected the line.

Two detectives arrived at my front door in less than ten minutes.

"Mr. Thompson, you need to come with me to release the man detained in your trunk," Detective Williams said in a huff.

I followed them out the door and watched as they guided the mystery man out of the trunk. As soon as he was upright, the detective handcuffed him.

"Who are you?" Detective Williams asked gruffly.

"I want an attorney," said the mystery man.

"Did you get his name?" the detective asked Jed and me.

"No, but he knows where my kids are," I said. "He said he ran away because he didn't want to see what they were going to do to Emily, Ellen, and Ryan."

"Is that so?" asked Detective Williams as he looked at the mystery man.

The only answer from the mystery man was a shrug of his shoulders. The detective turned him around and walked him out to a waiting patrol car.

"Take him in and book him for kidnapping," Williams instructed the officer.

Detective Williams returned to my house with Jed and me following him.

"Where was this guy when you found him?"

"We were following him after he ran past my car," said Jed. "Lindsay saw him first as he came running from the direction of the Greene house."

"Did you see him leave the Greene house?" he asked me.

"No, I saw him running from that direction," I answered. "Why can't you go inside the house and check it out since it is a crime scene already? Furthermore, why is my house cordoned off as a crime scene?"

"You can take that down. We don't need that up anymore," he said. "And we will go into the Greene house and check it out. I'm waiting for word from our Forced Entry Team."

"When do you expect to hear from them?" asked Jed.

"Any time now. They had to get set up and positioned around the house. A couple of the close neighbors had to be evacuated. It does take some time to get that all done."

The detective, Jed, and I were silent as we awaited the signal from the Forced Entry Team. I assumed it would be in the form of a call to Detective Williams's cell phone.

I didn't hear it ring, but it must have done so, because he reached inside his coat pocket and said, "Detective Williams."

He was suddenly up from the chair on which he was sitting and headed out the door.

"You two stay here," he commanded.

Chapter 11

I looked at Jed, and we both stood up. We walked to the front door, pulling it open slowly. Jed peeked out first and saw a uniformed police officer run in front of my house with his gun up and ready to fire.

"Back up, Linds," said Jed softly so he wouldn't be heard by anyone except me. "A cop just ran by with his gun at the ready. Maybe we should lock the door and get down low behind the furniture."

That scared me. I dropped to the floor and crawled behind the sofa. Jed took a position behind the loveseat, and we waited.

The minutes tick off the clock ever so slowly.

We heard no gunfire, but we heard heavy footsteps passing between the houses. We didn't know if the foot sounds belonged to the good guys or the bad guys, so we continued to hide and wait.

There was a knock at my front door.

"Who is it?" I shouted from behind the sofa.

"Williams," was the response.

Jed, who was closer to the door, rose up and turned the lock.

"Your kids weren't there," Williams said as soon as he entered the living room. "They had been there, but they were moved to another location, and they were still alive."

"How do you know they had been there?" I asked.

"Emily wrote her name in the dust on one of the tables. There was no sign of blood anywhere, so I'm sure they are still alive. Also, there were fast food wrappings all over the place to indicate several people had been in the house."

"Thank God, Emily left a sign," I said.

"Now what?" Jed asked.

"I need to talk to the man we arrested," Williams said.

"What if he doesn't tell you anything? Then what?" Jed asked.

"I will speak with his court appointed attorney, and we will go from there," the detective explained. "I'm going back to the office, and we will try to track down the culprits and your kids, Ms. Harris. I promise you, we will find them."

"I'm going to hold you to that promise," I said as I held back the storm of tears that had been building up. "Jed, where could they have moved my kids? Why didn't we see them do it?"

"They probably did it while we were chasing the mystery man," Jed said. "That may have been the reason he was running. They wanted us to chase him so they could sneak out of the house. I guess we fell for that little trick, but don't give up, Linds."

"I'm not giving up, Jed. I'm just afraid of what they might be doing to my girls and Ryan. I want to know why they needed to take them. All I could figure out is that the kids must have seen something they shouldn't have, and it must have happened at the Greene house."

"I think you're right about that, Linds. Do you know if Otis Greene was into anything illegal?" Jed asked.

"No, I wouldn't know that, but the kids might have heard something through the rumor mill."

"I bet they did," said Jed.

"All I know about Otis Greene is that he was mean and hateful," I said. "I couldn't get a pleasant word out of him, so I gave up trying to be friendly."

"What did he do that was so mean and hateful?" asked Jed.

"When the kids were playing and a ball or something landed in his yard, he wouldn't let them have it back to continue playing. He always told them to go on home. When I went over to retrieve whatever they lost in his yard, he cussed at me, told me to control my kids, and get off his property."

"Did that happen often?"

"No, they moved on up the street away from his house so their ball couldn't possibly land in his yard anymore. Ellen told me when she was talking with him, he put his hands where he shouldn't have touched her."

"Did you report that to the police?" Jed asked.

"No, she didn't tell me about it until after he died."

"Wow, that's a shame. He could have been gone and out of here long before the kids were taken, and this wouldn't have happened."

"Yeah, maybe, but Ellen didn't want me to get mad at her for talking with him," I continued.

"You've got some great kids. You know that, don't you?"

"Yes, I guess I'm lucky about having such great kids, but I want them back home with me and out of danger."

"Me too," agreed Jed.

33

Chapter 12

"Jed, I think we need to go talk with Marvin Mason," I said.

"Who is Marvin Mason?" Jed asked.

"He is a neighbor to Otis Greene. He might have seen them leave. He would be more likely to talk with us than the police. He is an elderly man who doesn't want any trouble."

"Okay, let's go talk to Marvin right now."

"Don't get belligerent with him, Jed. He is an old man, and I don't want him intimidated to silence, if you know what I mean."

"You can do the talking, Linds. I'll follow your lead."

We left the house, again. Thankful for something to do. The snow had stopped falling, but it was really cold. We didn't take the car because the Greene house was well within walking distance.

I walked up to Marvin Mason's front porch and gently tapped on his door. When I received no response, I knocked a bit harder. I heard a voice ask me who I was.

"It's Lindsay Harris, Mr. Mason. I talked to you earlier about my missing daughter!" I shouted so he could hear me clearly.

"Just a minute," he said weakly as he turned locks and released the chain. "What do you want now?"

"We, my friend Jed and I, are looking for all three of my kids," I said as I motioned for Jed to come onto the porch. "We wanted to know if you saw anyone leave your neighbor's house with two teenage girls and a young boy?"

There was silence.

"Please, Mr. Mason, we are trying to find my kids so I can take them home to celebrate Christmas," I pleaded.

"I did see a bunch of people leave there a while ago, but I don't think they saw me," Mr. Mason said. "At least, I hope they didn't see me." Once again, he started to look around to see if anyone was watching him or could hear him.

"Do you know which way they went?" asked Jed.

"They turned that way," he said as he pointed to the left.

"Did you see the car?" asked Jed.

"They climbed into two different cars. Both of them were old and beat up junkers. One was dark red, and the other one was silver or gray."

"You didn't get a plate number, did you?" I asked.

"No. No, I didn't see one on the cars. They might have had one, but I didn't see it. Bad eyes, you know."

"That's fine, Mr. Mason," I said. "You were a lot of help. We're going to drive around to see if we can find two old junkers parked somewhere. Thank you for your help." I turned to walk away.

"Young lady?"

"Yes, sir?"

"Will you let me know when you find your children?" asked Marvin Mason.

"I will make sure I do that personally, Mr. Mason. I hope

to see you real soon."

I turned to Jed to whisper, "Jed, let's go cruising," when we neared the car.

Chapter 13

It was getting colder, and I was worried about my children being in the frigid weather, being hungry and scared. It was getting close to Christmas, and I wanted my family with me to celebrate.

The snowflakes were, once again, flying. That was making my anxiety rise through the roof.

"How much longer do you want me to drive around?" asked Jed as he stifled a yawn.

"Until I find those cars," I snapped.

"Linds, chill out," said Jed.

"I'm so sorry, but I'm so worried," I replied.

"I know, but we are both getting tired," said Jed.

"Over there!" I said as I pointed to my right.

"Where?"

"Behind that old house. The one that has been empty for years," I said as I continued to point.

He pulled the car to the curb and continued to search the area with his eyes.

"Don't you see the cars?" I asked.

"Yes, yes, now I do. They are old, beat-up junkers for sure," he agreed.

"We need to check them out, don't you think?" I asked. The adrenaline rush came over me, and I was ready to go kidnapper hunting.

"Linds, wait a minute!" Jed said as I opened the car door.

"No, I need to check these cars. There might be something in there that belongs to one of the kids. Come on, let's look," I said excitedly.

As I climbed from the passenger seat and stood up, something whizzed past my ear.

"What was that?" I screamed.

"Someone's shooting at us! Get in the car...we've got to get out of here." Jed tried to hurry me along.

I moved toward the car, and another shot rang out from some unknown shooter. I grabbed my shoulder when I realized the bullet hit me.

"Get in here, now!" shouted Jed. "I'm taking you to the emergency room."

Suddenly, I felt the pain. Oh my gosh, did that hurt. The sight of blood and my crying because of the pain was making me lightheaded. I blinked my eyes rapidly as I tried to stay conscious.

"I'm about to pass out," I whispered weakly.

"Stay with me, Linds. Keep your eyes open, please," pleaded Jed. He was pressing way too hard on the gas pedal.

"Slow down," I whispered. "These roads are much too curvy for the speed you are driving."

"We're almost there. I can't slow down now!" he snapped at me.

"Okay..." I muttered as I passed out.

I roused up a little when Jed tried to pull me from the car.

"Stay awake, Linds," he pleaded. "We are at the emergency room right now."

"Okay," I whispered.

I don't remember much about the emergency room. When I came back to reality, I was in a hospital room with a police man standing in front of me. Jed was sitting in a chair, staring at me. I had no idea how long he had been waiting for me to awaken.

"Ms. Harris, who shot you?" asked the very professional police officer.

"I don't know," I whispered weakly.

"Do you have any enemies?" continued the officer.

"I've been searching for my children because they were kidnapped. We must be getting too close to finding them," I said as I felt myself begin to fade.

When I awakened again, Jed told me that he filled the police officer in on my missing children. I hoped the legal authorities would help me find them.

Chapter 14

Again, the lights ceased to exist in my head because I had passed out.

I had no idea how long those fits of darkness were lasting or how much time had passed since I entered the emergency room. I did know I had to get off that bed and into the car so I could look for my kids.

I didn't know how I was going to thank Jed for hanging in here with me. He has always been such a great friend.

"Jed," I whispered when I roused myself up again from the dark world of unconsciousness. "I need to get out of here to find my kids."

"You can't, not right now," Jed replied calmly. "The cops are looking for them, and I don't want you to get shot again. The next time, they might kill you. You don't want that, do you?"

"Of course not, but I want to find Ellen, Emily, and Ryan. If you're not going to help me, then leave," I said angrily as I grimaced in pain.

"I'm not going anywhere, Linds," Jed said as he tried to soothe my temper. "I'm staying right by your side until your kids are home safely."

"I really need to get out of here, Jed," I cried as I held onto my painful shoulder.

"I'll go and see if I can find the doctor. I'll ask him about how soon you will be released." He stood to leave the room.

I needed to get out of there. It really didn't matter what the doctor told Jed; I was getting out of there.

I passed out again, and when I woke, a stranger was standing in front of me.

He was glancing around as if he were looking for someone, or afraid he was going to be caught doing something he shouldn't be doing.

"Who are you?" I asked in a raspy voice.

"Are you the lady who is looking for her kids?"

"Yes, I am. Do you know where they are being held?" I asked excitedly. "Tell me your name, please."

My hold on reality was beginning to waiver. I wasn't sure that what I was seeing was real.

Did I see a gun in that man's hand? I asked myself as my world turned black again.

When I woke up, my room was filled with people.

Jed told me he had come into the room, and the man was holding a gun. He was followed by a nurse who was trying to dispense medication. The doctor came in next, and Jed grabbed the strange man's gun. There was a scuffle, and a security guard with his gun drawn entered the room. The security guard escorted everyone out of the room except for the doctor and nurse.

All of that happened while I was out cold. I was then taken to an operating room, where the bullet was removed from my shoulder.

The bullet was the reason I kept passing out.

Chapter 15

When I returned from surgery, I roused myself back into reality. I looked around. I didn't see the man with the gun, but Jed was asleep in a chair.

"Was that real?" I muttered.

Jed must have heard me, because he also roused himself and saw that I was awake.

"Jed, are you awake?" I whispered.

"Yes, how are you feeling?" he asked.

I didn't know how to answer that question because I wasn't sure how I was feeling after being drugged for surgery, other than being grateful that I was still alive.

"Linds, are you okay?"

I blinked my eyes several times as I tried to clear the haze from my eyes and mind from the anesthesia.

"Yeah, I think so, but I need to know what the doctor said my prognosis would be," I said with a drugged slur in my voice.

"You can leave tomorrow if you don't have any problems tonight," Jed explained. "I told him why it was so important for you to leave, and he agreed to release you tomorrow, begrudgingly. He wants you to wear a sling so you will refrain

42

from using your injured shoulder."

"I'll be glad to wear a sling if I can get out of here and look for my babies," I said as I stifled the tears that were welling up in my eyes again.

Well, I did have problems. The pain was excruciating, and the blood began to flow through the bandages. I didn't want to say anything to anyone, but the moaning was a giveaway. I didn't realize I was emitting any sounds, but they did slip out when I was trying to sleep. Of course, the nurse saw the blood and called for the doctor to check out the wound.

"Can't you just give me a pain pill? I need to get out of here tomorrow," I begged the tall, older man who proclaimed himself to be Dr. Swanson.

"We will answer that question when daylight breaks," he said calmly.

The bleeding stopped after the dressing was changed. The pain diminished when an injection of medicine was added to my IV. I was quiet for the rest of the night because I entered into a drug induced sleep.

When I awoke the next morning, Jed was sitting in a chair beside my bed.

"Did you get any sleep, Jed?" I asked.

"Yeah, I drove to your house and slept on the sofa," he said. "It was quite comfortable. I called into work and told then what was happening, and they told me to take all of the time I needed. You know I will have to write about this after we find the kids."

"I know, and I am so grateful for your help," I answered. "But—I need to get out of here."

43

Chapter 16

"I'm out of here," I whispered to Jed after I managed to get dressed.

"Where to? Home, I hope," Jed said as he took my free arm to lead me to the wheelchair that would roll me to the car.

"Let's look for the kids."

"I knew you were going to say that, but I'm going to get the car. I'll bring it around to the front, but give me a couple of minutes to clean the snow off the windshield." Jed rushed out the door, allowing the nurse to escort me to the main lobby to wait.

The snow was falling faster than Jed could remove it, but he tried. He pulled up under the hospital entrance, and I climbed into the almost warm vehicle.

We slid around a bit in the parking lot as Jed tried to drive to the street.

"It's dangerous out here, Linds. I think I should take you home," Jed said sternly.

"No, no, please take me to the street where the house is and where they held the kids. I want to find my children," I said just as sternly as Jed.

44

"Okay, okay," he replied.

I did not say another word to him as he struggled to navigate the icy, snow-covered roads. He needed to concentrate on driving and not worry about me.

A car was driving toward us, and it was sliding more than Jed. Actually, it was headed straight for us, but it hit a patch of ice and swerved away precariously.

"Do you recognize the driver?" asked Jed.

"No—do you?" I asked.

"He was coming straight at us," Jed said with fear in his voice. "I'm so glad he hit that patch of ice and slid into the guardrail; otherwise, we would be dead meat."

"We need to follow him to find the kids, but we also need to go on driving ahead and hide somewhere so we can turn around to have him lead the way," I said with excitement coloring my tone.

"That's a good idea, Linds, but where can we hide?" asked Jed.

"I don't know, just keep driving. I'm sure we can find a place, and I'm also sure he will keep following us so he can finish the killing job." The excitement faded in my voice, and the extraordinary fear returned.

"Just keep driving is easier said than done on these icy, snow-covered roads, but I will try," said Jed as he kept his eyes glued to the road in front of us.

The snow was falling faster and obliterating our vision of the road in front of us. If we were having a hard time navigating the onslaught of nature, I was sure they were having the same problem.

"Turn off your headlights and taillights. It will make it a lot harder to follow us if they can't see us," I suggested.

When the lights were extinguished, Jed found it harder to drive, but he kept at it until he saw a driveway that led to an abandoned house. He made a quick right turn, and we prayed that wind would blow snow over the tracks so our follower wouldn't know that we had left the main road.

We cowered down as much as possible so our follower wouldn't be able to tell if the car was occupied or not.

The wait was everlasting, or at least it seemed like it, but finally we thought we might be able to pull out of the driveway and start following the prospective killer.

We had heard a vehicle pass us and then turn around to drive past us again.

Jed drove slowly because the snow was building up on the road and covering the patches of ice.

The car went into a severe slide, and I thought we were going to have a major accident, but Jed managed to get out of the ice that caused that problem.

We proceeded on with the fear of God accentuated in our heads and hearts. We were crossing a bridge to continue the chase, but that was a major problem. We slid into the guardrail initially, but Jed managed to back up the vehicle enough to try to go forward. We drove a few feet and slid again, then into the guardrail again.

With the second slide, Jed was getting angry. That was when the third slide happened. He backed out and away from the guardrail again and cursed the designer of the bridge for building it at such an angle that would promote these slides.

We were finally off the bridge without any apparent damage to the vehicle, but our minds took a major hit.

"The roads are getting really bad," whispered Jed as he struggled to stay on what he thought was pavement.

"I know. Maybe we should go home. If we both get killed, no one will look for the kids," I said as I fought back tears.

"We'll look again when this snowstorm lets up," said Jed with all the sincerity he could muster.

Chapter 17

Jed helped me into the house. He was afraid I would fall and break something else, but I fooled him. I didn't fall until I got to the living room, where I fell onto the sofa.

"You had better get some rest. We can look for the kids in the morning," said Jed as he tried to keep me from venturing out again into the snowy weather.

"I guess you're right," I said in a fading tone. "I do need to rest...but we go out looking first thing in the morning, okay?"

Jed helped me up from the sofa so I could get him some sheets to spread on the sofa so he could get some sleep, too.

It was a long night. The pain from my wound was unrelenting. It would wake me as soon as I slipped into a deeper sleep. Continuous sleep was not possible. I made myself stay in bed so I wouldn't bother Jed.

I checked the time every few minutes as the moments passed ever so slowly. The worry about my kids never stopped. I was so afraid they would be molested or even killed. I saw it happening in my dreams. I woke up screaming and Jed came running into my room to see what was wrong.

48

"Lindsay, Lindsay, wake up," Jed said softly. "You're having a nightmare."

I blinked my eyes quickly as I tried to get my brain to focus on Jed standing in front of me. I started to cry uncontrollably, shaking all over.

"Linds, wake up please, and tell me what's wrong," pleaded Jed.

"The kids...I saw them molest and kill my babies," I said between sobs.

"No, Linds, it was only a dream. We are going to find your kids today. I promise you that we will find them today," Jed said as he held me close so I would stop shaking.

I nudged him away from me so I could get off the bed and get ready to go searching.

"Let's go," I whispered. "We can grab some coffee at a fast-food place. We might even grab a bite to eat. We need to take it with us so we can search."

Outside, we were surprised that the streets had been plowed and were now passable.

Jed helped me to the passenger side of the vehicle. He then ran to the driver's side, started the engine, and let it run while he brushed the snow away from all windows.

After ordering coffee and a handheld breakfast item, we were off to start the search again.

49

Chapter 18

I looked up at the sky to check for clouds. They were there, and they were dark and angry looking.

"I hope it doesn't snow anymore," I whispered to Jed.

"Don't get your hopes up. The flakes are starting to fly now," he said in response.

"We just can't catch a break," I mumbled with exasperation as I fought the tears again.

"Look, over there," said Joe as he motioned to his right.

"Where?" I asked as I strained to see what he was talking about.

"That house has a light on inside," he said excitedly.

"Okay, why is that special?" I asked softly.

"It is an abandoned house. No one has lived in it or years. At least, that's what I've been told."

"Why would you even know that?"

"I was planning to do a story on abandoned houses in Virginia. That was one I was asking about."

"Turn around, and let's go check it out," I said sternly.

"I was planning to do just that," said Jed.

Jed made a quick right turn into someone's driveway, where

he backed the car out onto the street and headed for the so-called abandoned house.

"I don't see the light," I whispered.

"That's okay," Jed said softly. "We know someone was there. They haven't had time to get very far."

"You're going past it," I said.

"I know, I know. I don't want them to see me checking up on them. I'm going to park a couple of houses away along the street."

I started to reach for the door handle so I could exit the vehicle.

"You stay here, Linds," he commanded. "I don't want you to get hurt any more than you already are."

I looked at him and felt all of the air leave my body. I wanted to go with him, but I was also thankful that he told me to stay put. The pain did not want to go away. I settled myself back into my seat to wait.

"Dear God, I hate to wait," I mumbled. Waiting and the patience to wait were not virtues of mine.

I tried to keep a watchful eye out for Jed, but I was sitting with my back toward the front of the abandoned house. Despite the worry that was filling my mind, I was getting so very tired. My eyes were heavy, and it was difficult for me to focus.

Suddenly the car door opened, and Jed jumped in with his keys in hand to start the car. He slammed the gearshift into drive and took off like the devil was on his tail.

"What's wrong, Jed?" I screamed at him.

"Gunfire!" he shouted as he swerved the vehicle from side to side.

I could hear the pop of gunfire, but I couldn't see who was shooting at us.

"Why, Jed?" I sputtered.

"I saw the kids, and they saw me," he said as he pressed harder on the gas pedal.

The car started to slide, but he pulled it out and continued on up the road.

"Are they chasing us?" I asked fearfully.

"No, I don't see them. I'm racing to the police department before they have a chance to load up and leave."

"I have my cell phone. I'll call them."

I pressed the digits 9-1-1.

Chapter 19

The sirens were blaring when the police cars pulled to a stop after seeing Jed wave at them.

"Can you stop the sirens and flashing lights?" I pleaded. "You will cause them to panic, and they might harm my children."

"Where are your children?" asked the policeman, who was standing in front of my side of the car.

"At the abandoned house a few blocks ahead," I said. "My friend Jed can show you where the house is located. Please get my children away from those people so we can celebrate Christmas as a family." Once again, I fought back the tears.

"Take a deep breath, lady. We will find your kids," said the sympathetic police officer.

The police did as I asked by eliminating the flashing lights. Jed jumped into one of the police vehicles and directed them to the abandoned house. A second patrol car pulled over in front of me and told me to get into the car in the front passenger seat. He drove slowly to where he spotted the other police vehicle that Jed had been in while searching for the abandoned house.

"Stay here, ma'am," the officer said. "I'm going to check on what's happening." He exited the car with his gun drawn and at the ready.

"What's the gun for? My kids are in there," I sputtered.

Too late. He was off and running to the side of the house.

"What is going on?" I mumbled as I struggled to get out of the car. My arm was still in a sling and not allowing me any type of support.

I was finally standing erect, so I started to walk to the side of the house where I saw the police officer disappear around a corner.

He wasn't there, but I could hear voices. I turned from side to side, trying to locate the sounds. They seemed to be bouncing off of everything that was solid. I strained my hearing to make out some of the words, but they were all muddled.

I walked toward the voices. I thought they seemed to be farther behind the house toward the back yard. My shoulder was beginning to really hurt. I guessed it was because I was holding it in a strain as I tried to hurry myself along to find these voices.

I finally spotted the police officer, and he looked a little shaken. I approached him slowly.

"What's wrong?" I asked softly.

The officer did not answer me.

"Tell me what is wrong, please," I whispered.

"10..." he mumbled into the transmitter he had pulled from the front of his shirt.

"What does that mean?" I asked.

"That means I need back up, now," he sputtered.

"Why?" I asked as my voice was getting louder and rising.

He didn't answer me, so I started to walk in the direction from which he had come.

"Stop, lady! You can't go back there!" the officer shouted.

I paid no mind to his command. I kept going because I needed to see what was back there. The officer came running after me and grabbed my shoulder.

"Stop! That hurts!" I shouted.

I stopped walking when I saw the body. I could see it wasn't Jed or one of my children, but I didn't recognize the man.

Chapter 20

"Do you recognize that man lying there?" asked the officer.
"No—no I don't. I have no idea who he is or why he's dead," I answered with emphasis on the negative.

"Is he one of the persons who took your kids?"

"I don't know. I never saw who took them. They just disappeared."

"What do you mean they just disappeared?"

"Otis Greene, our neighbor, was murdered, so my kids were snooping around trying to find clues. Then, they were gone," I explained.

"They shouldn't have been doing that. That is a job for the police," scolded the officer.

"I know, I know, but he was our neighbor, and we just wanted to help," I said as I winced from a pain running through my shoulder and arm. I tried to readjust my position to relieve the pain.

"What happened to you that put your arm in a sling?" asked the curious officer.

"Someone shot me."

"Who?"

"I don't know...It might have been the man on the ground in front of us," I said sarcastically. I was getting tired of the interrogation.

Another police officer rounded the corner to offer a helping hand.

"Did you see another man go around this house?" I asked rapidly. "He is my friend Jed, and now he is gone and missing."

"No, the only one I saw is lying right here on the ground," the new officer mumbled before snapping, "What was your friend looking for at the back of the house?"

"My kids. He was looking for my kids!" I screamed as the tears started to flow.

"You need to go sit down, ma'am," said the officer.

"No, no, I don't. I need to find Jed and my kids, Emily, Ellen, and Ryan."

"We'll do the looking," said the first officer.

I turned to leave. As soon as they got the body removed and out of the way, I was going to go back and do some snooping of my own, again.

The crime scene tape was renewed, and the area was completely blocked from spectators. The coroner arrived and unceremoniously scooped up the dead body. The police officers searched the house and discovered no one was inside, but they stayed for a long time, gathering evidence.

I had been sitting on a metal chair on my front porch when I saw the last of them leave.

It was almost dark, and I knew I really shouldn't be walking around that house alone. I decided to go inside my house and wait until morning to continue my search for my kids and my friend.

Chapter 21

The night was long, and sleep was intermittent because of the pain. I could not find comfort when I was lying on my bed. I rose from the extreme discomfort and went to the recliner, searching for relief. The pain would not go away. It would dull a little but never go away. When I did drift off to sleep, I awoke with a start because of the nightmare that filtered into my mind.

The nightmare was explicit. It showed me how each of my children were killed. Jed hadn't entered the nightmare yet, but I was sure he would because he was my best friend.

I finally forced myself up from the recliner and went in search of a plastic bag to cover my shoulder. I was going to take a shower to help revive me and hopefully ease some of the pain.

I stood under the spray of warm water, and I could feel myself come out of the deep, dark hole of pain and despair. When I climbed out of the shower, I began the one-handed process of getting dressed and out to search for my missing people.

The sun was up, but many clouds were floating across the sky, creating an unwanted darkness that was telling me more snow was coming. The gloom did not help my faltering disposition.

I struggled into my jeans and carefully shrugged into a sweatshirt after I removed the sling. I put my arm back into the sling because it was too painful to let it hang down with no support. I put my free right arm into a jacket, letting the left side surround my shoulder.

My shoes were easy to slip on, but I knew I couldn't deal with boots of any kind.

I left my house through the back door so that anyone out front keeping an eye on the Greene house and its surroundings wouldn't see me leave.

I knew the criminals had left the Greene house, but I needed to know where they went and, hopefully, there might be some kind of sign to point me into the right direction.

The gloom outside was making it difficult to see anything inside the Greene house. I didn't bring a flashlight, because if anyone was outside watching, they would see the shine.

I looked through each room, and in the last room I entered, it finally gave me a sign. At least, I thought it was a sign. There was a butterfly scratched into the wall with what looked like blood.

"Emily, thank you," I whispered as I turned to leave.

I walked out of the Greene house, keeping close to the walls so no one could see me. I scrambled out the back door and into my house, where I grabbed my handbag and the second set of car keys. Jed had the first set in his pocket.

I started driving toward the street where the girls lived that collected butterflies. They weren't real butterflies, but they were all brightly colored and good collector items.

I turned onto the street and drove slowly past all of the houses, gazing at the vehicles in the driveways and, whenever possible, looking into the interiors where there were windows with the curtains slightly parted.

All of the houses had some exposure, except one that was closed up tight so no one could see inside. That was the one I wanted to check out.

Chapter 22

I kept driving past the house I wanted to investigate. I pulled the car over to the side of the road up on the grass so that people could get by me without damaging either vehicle.

My next challenge was to get off of the driver's seat without doing more damage to my sore shoulder. When I crawled into the car, the pain was bad. It finally settled down a bit, but then I had to climb out of the car. That was going to stir up the pain again.

"Let's go, Linds," I mumbled as I reached across my body to release the door latch.

The only thing I was grateful for with the injury was the fact that it was my left shoulder that was wounded. I needed my right shoulder to help me drive, but it was still painful to climb in and out of the car.

"Oh well, Linds, get over it," I told myself as I struggled with the climb, trying not to put any pressure on my sore shoulder. The pain radiated down my arm when I moved it in certain directions, so I tried not to move it.

Finally, I was out of the car and upright so I could walk to the house and look around to see if I could find my kids and Jed.

Walking seemed to be difficult. I guessed it was because I was still weak from the gunshot and loss of blood. I had to keep going. I had to check out the house.

There were no cars parked in the driveway, so I was losing hope. I needed to be brave, so I walked up the front sidewalk and climbed the steps that led to the porch, where I knocked on the door. Of course, no one came to answer the door. I expected that to happen.

I left the front porch and walked around to the back of the house with the idea that I would knock on the back door. That was easier said than done.

There was a gate and a fenced-in yard that contained two huge dogs. They were not happy to see me. They barked furiously at me and bared their teeth in anticipation of tearing me apart piece by piece.

I backed away from the gate and made my way to a window, where I tried to look inside the room in which it was located. I cupped my left hand to shade my eyes from the glare of the sunless day.

I could see absolutely nothing. The room appeared to be without furniture.

"What is going on?" I mumbled as I walked to the next window.

Again, nothing. No furniture, no pictures on the wall, and no one living in that house whatsoever.

I proceeded to walk to the other side of the house for further snooping into the contents of the structure. I would have called it a home, but that title certainly didn't fit.

I heard a car driving along the road, so I stood still as close to the house as I could get. I was so cold that I was beginning to shake. I stood there for what seemed like forever, but the car finally moved on, and I did the same thing.

I went to my car just in time for the snow to begin to fall. While the white flakes were beautiful, they were also dangerous as they began to accumulate. I started the car and turned the heater to full blast. I needed to get warmer any way that I could to stop the shaking.

I couldn't see the kids or Jed in that house, but they still could have been in an area that was too dark for my eyes to penetrate. I couldn't see where the cars had gone that contained my family and Jed, but I wasn't giving up the search.

The police department wasn't telling me anything. I was sure they were working on the disappearance, but they weren't talking with me. My mind whirled around and stopped on the television station.

"That's what I need to do. I need to let everyone in this little town know what's happening all around them."

Chapter 23

I searched the Internet for the local television station. My plan was to send what little information I had to each of the news anchors to get an invitation to be interviewed.

My email read:

My three children are missing, along with my friend who was helping me look for them. Is it possible for me to appear on your broadcast to ask for help with finding four missing people? Your prompt reply would be appreciated.
— Lindsay Harris

I waited.
I worried.
I waited.
Finally!
The response from Ally Marshall was short and very welcomed.

Would you be able to appear on the 5 p.m. show for an interview?
— Ally Marshall

My response was as follows:

Yes, please tell me what time to be there!

Her response said 3 p.m. That didn't give me much time to get myself together, but I said I would be there.

I took a shower, and that was difficult with my extremely sore shoulder. Washing my hair was a one-armed, painful task. I had to let my hair air dry while I dressed in clothing that was easy to get onto my body.

I hurried to my car and discovered the snow was falling again. Normally, I would be happy to see the snow, but being a one-armed driver prevented me from enjoying the beauty.

Christmas was only three days away, and I was trying so hard to get my family and friend back to enjoy the season. I started my car, turned the heat up as far as it would go, and waited for everything to melt off my windows.

When I was able to see whatever was ahead of me, I put the car into gear and started driving to the television station. I knew the exact location because I had passed it many times while on my way to work.

The roads were becoming snow covered, so I had to slow my speed, but I was determined to get there on time.

I turned onto the driveway at 3 p.m. on the dot. I made my way to the front of the building and entered the waiting area, where a receptionist was located. The receptionist placed a quiet call, and a tall, dark-haired lady appeared from around a corner.

"Hi. I'm Ally Marshall, and you must be Lindsay Harris?" she said as she extended her hand for a friendly shake.

"Yes, I'm Lindsay," I said with enthusiasm, because I really felt the interview might help me locate the missing people.

Ally talked with me for a few moments and went away to prepare for the 5 p.m. broadcast. She told me that she would come and take me to the studio before 5 p.m., and I would wait there until my interview time.

As the time approached, I was thinking about what I would say. Then, I decided I needed Ally to lead me.

"This is a special interview with a lady who has family members and a friend missing from her world," Ally began. "Her name is Lindsay Harris, and she is here to tell us what happened. Lindsay, tell me how and when your children disappeared."

"One at a time, my two daughters, Emily and Ellen, disappeared. They were stationed in different places," I said. "I don't know exactly when they left, but both were gone within an hour. My son, Ryan, was gone soon after."

"Did you see anyone around that may have looked suspicious?" asked Ally.

"No, ma'am, I saw no one. That's why it's so mysterious," I answered.

"You said they were stationed. What do you mean by that?" asked Ally.

"My girls and son wanted to know why a neighbor was murdered. I didn't want them to go near the house, so I said they had to stay on the front porch or back porch of our house to watch the comings and goings around us. They were enticed to leave the porches, but I don't know who or what enticed them."

"Your three children all disappeared. What about your friend?" asked Ally.

"Jed was helping look for my children, and then he was

gone," I said. "I can't find any of them, and I'm desperately seeking help from everyone." I tried to stop my tears.

"You have a bandaged shoulder, and your arm is in a sling. What happened?" asked Ally.

"The monsters who kidnapped my children shot me when I was trying to find them to bring them back home. Christmas is so close, and I wanted them there to share the joys with me."

"How can we help?" asked Ally.

I pulled photographs from my handbag and handed them to Ally. She passed them on to the camera man, who was focused on them.

"If anyone sees any of these four people, please call 9-1-1 and tell them where you saw them," I said. "Please help!" My tears could not be controlled now.

Ally walked me out to the waiting area and thanked me for appearing on the broadcast. She gave me a hug and wished me good luck in finding my family and Jed.

Chapter 24

I walked out into the falling snow, entered my car, and just sat there trying to figure out what to do next.

I started the engine, and the warmth from the heater caused me to close my eyes. I don't know how long I slept, but I didn't wake up until someone pounded on the window while brushing at the snow.

"Lindsay, are you okay?" asked Ally.

"Yes, I guess I am," I said slowly.

"Why are you still here?" she asked. "What happened?"

"I really don't know," I answered as I tried to look around to get my bearings.

"Are you feeling okay?" Ally asked again.

"No, I feel like I may lose it again from all the pain," I said as fast as I could because I could feel my voice becoming fainter.

"I'm calling 9-1-1," Ally said. "You really need some help."

I heard what she said, I think, as my eyes closed and my mind went totally blank.

When I opened my eyes, I was in the emergency room of the local hospital, where I was hooked up to an IV and my nose was invaded by an oxygen tube.

"What happened?" I asked the nurse as she entered the curtained cubicle.

"An ambulance brought you here because you were totally unconscious in your car," said the nurse as she took my blood pressure.

"What are you treating me for? What is wrong with me?" I asked.

"Your doctor will be in here in a few minutes. He can tell you all about it," the nurse said as she pulled the curtain aside to leave the area.

I needed an answer, but when I tried to move, my shoulder hurt so very much, and it caused me to let a moan escape.

"Ms. Harris, you need to refrain from moving around too much," said an ordinary-looking man wearing a white coat with the name Dr. John Hudson emblazoned above the breast pocket. "Your shoulder is very infected."

"Why am I here?" I asked sternly.

"The infection in your bullet wound was making you very sick," he explained. "You should have seen your doctor a couple of days ago. Just to let you know, I had to contact the legal authorities about the bullet wound. It's a legal obligation."

"They already know about it," I snapped back at him.

As soon as my mouth closed from that snappish comment, a uniformed policeman pushed the curtain aside.

"Ms. Harris, we have been looking for you," said the officer.

"I've been looking for my kids, like you should be," I said as I tried to control the words that I wanted to say.

"We have been looking for your children and your friend. We have a couple of leads that we are checking out," said the officer.

"When will you tell me anything other than you have a couple of leads?" I demanded.

"Ms. Harris, that's all I can tell you right now. We will be in touch with you as soon as we learn more." The officer left the curtained cubicle.

"Thanks for nothing," I mumbled as the curtain stopped moving after his departure.

The nurse stepped back in the curtained cubicle. She had a concerned look.

"Is he gone yet?" I asked.

"Yes, Ms. Harris," the nurse said.

"Will the doctor be in here soon?" I asked as politely as I was able.

"Just a few more minutes. Are you having a lot of pain?" asked the concerned nurse.

"Yes, I am," I said.

"I'll try to get him in here as soon as possible," said the nurse as she pushed aside the curtain.

I waited impatiently for the doctor to make an appearance. I needed to get out and away from the emergency room to look for my family.

"Ms. Harris, the nurse said you are having a great deal of pain, which is to be expected with the amount of infection that set up in your wound," the doctor said at last. "As the infection dissipates, the pain will also fade. I will order some pain medication to get you through the hours that you are awake."

"When can I get out of here?" I asked in a not-too-polite tone.

"I thought we would go day by day because of the infection. It may become worse, in which case I would have to do surgery to remove the infected flesh."

"That won't do," I said angrily. "I have to get out of here because my kids and my friend have been kidnapped. I have to keep looking for them. I need to get out of here."

"I understand your dilemma. But you need to get that infection under control, or you too will become missing—permanently." The doctor emphasized *permanently*.

Chapter 25

The nurse reappeared and started the process of transporting me to a room.

I wanted to go to a room so I could unhook everything attached to me and leave the hospital with or without their permission. I was feeling woozy, and I was so afraid they were pumping medication into me that would knock me into dream land.

Finally, I was positioned in my room and checked on by the nurse who departed hurriedly to take care of another admission from the emergency room. I was fighting the attack of sleepiness, but I knew I was losing the battle. I closed my eyes, and I was asleep despite my protestations. The dreams started forming in my brain, and I had no choice but to be a part of the drama.

I was riding in the car in the passenger seat. Someone else was driving, but I couldn't see who it was. When I asked where we were going, the only answer I received was a grunt.

I stared ahead as I tried to see where we were going. Nothing looked familiar, but I was sure it wasn't very far from home. We continued to drive and we entered fog. The windshield was so foggy that it was like we were driving blind. I glimpsed at something I thought was familiar, but it was covered with fog so quickly that my mind couldn't figure out what I saw.

We drove on and on until there was a crash, and I opened my eyes. I looked around and tried to discern where I was. It certainly wasn't my bedroom. My mind finally started to climb from the sleep fog, and I was in a hospital room.

I had no idea whether it was day or night. I didn't know how many hours I had been asleep, but I wanted out of there.

I rose from my position on the hospital bed, and I realized there were medical tubes attached to me in my arm. I peeled the tape off the needle that was inserted in my vein and pushed down on the area where I could see the needle. I jerked the needle out quickly while I pushed down on my skin and vein to stop the bleeding. I kept the pressure on the point of insertion and hoped it would stop bleeding.

I had to hurry. I got off of my bed and started dressing. I didn't want the nurse to catch me and try to stop me from leaving. I was drugged and lightheaded when I stood up. I took a few deep breaths and continued searching for my personal items.

By the time I finally had my clothes in place, my shoulder was hurting really bad. I gritted my teeth to keep my mouth from yelling out from the pain. I opened the door to my room and peeked around it to see if the coast was clear.

There was activity at the nurses' station, but their attention was directed at the opposite end of the corridor. I stepped out into the corridor and walked to the exit that led to the stair-case. The elevator would have required me to walk to the area of activity. That wouldn't do, so I opted for the staircase.

I didn't know how long it would take for the medical staff to discover that I was among the missing. I wanted to be out of their reach when that happened. I was a bit disheveled in appearance, but that was okay. Not everyone who visited a friend or family member in the hospital was super tidy.

I reached the lobby/waiting area, and no one was looking for me—yet. I walked out the front door and spotted a cab. I briskly walked without drawing attention and stepped up to the rear door of the cab. When I managed to climb inside, I gave the cab driver my home address.

When he drove closer to my house, I saw a police car in the driveway.

"Sir, take me to the television station so I can retrieve my car," I said so he would steer clear of my house.

"Yes, ma'am," the driver responded politely.

I knew he had seen the police car. He drove on without question.

"There it is," I said as I pointed to my car parked in the television station parking lot.

He pulled the cab close and climbed from the driver seat to help me out of the back seat. I paid his fee and gave him a nice tip. He deserved it.

I climbed into my car and drove off to find my missing children and friend.

Chapter 26

I wanted to drive in front of my house, but I was afraid the police would see me. Instead, I chose to drive down the alley behind all of the houses on my street, where I found nothing that would help me.

My mind flashed back to the dream I had during my drug-induced sleep. I saw something, but I couldn't put my finger on what I saw.

"What did I see?" I mumbled as I kept driving.

I circled around the area for an hour, and there it was. I pulled my car over to the curb and waited. I stared at the name plate in the middle of the yard. Written in black letters against a bright white background was the name *Elkart*.

"My kids are in there," I mumbled as I positioned myself to get out of the car.

I turned my head to see if anyone was coming from the house. I returned to my driving position and pulled slowly away from the curb. I saw a big-bodied male walking out the doorway as he looked directly at my car.

"Oh no," I mumbled. "He saw me and knows who I am." I pushed the gas pedal to create some speed.

I saw no one behind me, so I drove into the parking lot of a chain supermarket and parked in the middle of a bunch of cars. I watched for a vehicle that appeared to be searching for someone. The SUV was driving slower than anyone else on the road. He was peering at the cars parked in the lot where I was located. I ducked down so he wouldn't be able to see me as I prayed that he would move on.

I stayed in the hunkered down position for what seemed like forever. My shoulder began to radiate pain, so I had to straighten up. I looked out the window, and I didn't see him anywhere. I breathed an enormous sigh of relief.

I drove to the police station and told them what had just happened.

Surprise, surprise. They took immediate action. A police car was sent to the address I had given. I waited and waited for an answer, but nothing came into the office. The officer who had been directed to check things out reported there was nothing and no one there.

I was livid, but I held my tongue. I wanted to scream and throw a tantrum, but I maintained my cool. I told the officer, when he returned to the station, that there had to be someone there who knew where my kids were located. If not, why was that man looking for me?

"For all I know, he was the one who shot me," I said to the officer.

When I mentioned that possibility to the officer, he took an interest in my story.

"What's your name?" I asked the officer.

"Officer Smith, and I'm really interested in trying to find your family," he said in a whisper.

"The detectives tell me every time I call or stop in the station

76

that they are working on it. I don't see any results at all, and I don't see my family," I said softly so that other people in the room couldn't hear me.

"Well, I will do what I can to help you, but I have to do it on the down low," he said. "I'm not a detective, and I'm sure those guys would resent my interference. So, I will call you every day and let you know what I have discovered. Don't call here and ask for me unless it is an emergency. Is that okay with you?"

"Sure, sure, anything you can do to help is fine with me," I sputtered.

Chapter 27

I left the police station with no news from the detectives, but I gained the interest of Officer Smith. Maybe he could get some answers that didn't seem to be reaching the detectives.

I drove in the direction that would take me home. The pain in my shoulder was growing fiercely with each passing minute. I glanced up to the rearview mirror and saw that SUV again.

"Dear God, why me!?" I shouted as I pushed the gas pedal to pick up more speed.

The SUV was looming larger and larger in my rearview mirror. I had to lose him, but I didn't know how to do that. I just kept driving, way too fast, but I continued to move...as did the SUV.

"There is never a cop around when you need one," I mumbled as I fought back tears.

As soon as my mouth slammed shut, I heard a faint screaming of a siren. The flashing lights and siren appeared suddenly behind the SUV. He had a choice to either try to outrun the law or pull over and face the consequences.

Despite the pain and stress, a smile appeared on my face as I drove on toward my home.

I pulled onto my driveway and into my garage. I didn't want anyone to see my car, especially the driver of the SUV. I had to have a break from driving and putting all of the strain onto my aching shoulder. I fell down onto the sofa when I reached the living room. A few moments passed, and I was in dream land again.

I saw the same house with "Elkart" printed on the sign in the front yard. In the distance, I could see shadows moving around beyond the curtains inside the house. The shadows were different shapes and sizes.

I knew my kids were in there, but I also knew this was merely a dream.

I struggled with trying to identify everyone from the shadow shape that appeared behind the curtains.

The smallest shadow was Ryan. The two girls were identical in size and shape, so I could identify them as Ellen and Emily. The tallest shadow was Jed.

There were other shadows that I knew had to be the captors. I saw two, possibly three, other shadows and shapes I did not recognize. There was a hint that one of the unidentified shadows was holding a handgun, and his arm was thrusting forward toward the people milling around in front of him. He kept pushing the gun forward, and the shadows kept backing away from the gun.

A *flash of fire came from the end of the gun.*

I woke up. I didn't know who was shot. I looked around me, trying to figure out where I was and what I was planning to do.

I tried to get up from the position in which I had fallen asleep. The pain was horrendous.

"When will it go away?" I mumbled as I cried. I continued to cry until I had no more tears streaming down my cheeks.

I forced myself up, pain or no pain, and headed outside to my car.

I needed to find the people missing from my life.

Chapter 28

I climbed into my car and stared at nothing. I wasn't focusing, and my mind was whirling around without stopping on anything.

I shook my head from side to side as I tried to stop the whirling of thoughts. Finally, my brain began to clear. I started my car. My cell phone started ringing, and I had to search through my handbag to find it. When I answered it, I didn't recognize the number, but I was afraid not to answer. It might be about my kids.

"Hello," I said weakly.

"Ms. Harris, this is Officer Smith."

"Yes, sir, do you have any information for me?"

"Yes, ma'am, I think I have your answer," he explained hurriedly. "If you will meet me at 331 Valleyview, I will get them out of there for you."

"Sure, sure, I'm in my car right now, and Valleyview is not very far from my house."

"Good, I'll meet you there. But if you get there before I do, wait for me."

"Okay."

The line disconnected, and I moved into action.

No more whirling thoughts and being unfocused. I was ready to find my three children and Jed.

Chapter 29

It didn't take me very long to get to Valleyview, and I didn't see Officer Smith anywhere.

I watched the house at 331. No one could be seen, so I wondered about the address. Maybe he gave me the wrong one. I wasn't parked in the driveway, but no other vehicle was parked there.

"What gives?" I mumbled as I continued to watch the house.

My gaze was focused on the front window, where I thought I saw the curtain move. I didn't see the person who walked up to my car and rapped on my window.

I lowered the window a bit and said, "Who are you?"

"Officer Smith sent me."

"Where is Officer Smith?" I asked skeptically.

"He's on his way. He wanted me to take you inside the house," the man said sternly.

"No, I don't think so," I said as I raised my window to the closed position.

This man didn't like that I closed the window, and he started beating on it and trying to make me open it again.

"Go away!" I shouted as I started my car to drive away.

He didn't like the sound of the engine revving as I put my car in gear, and I tromped on the gas pedal. Something wasn't right about this whole scene. Fortunately, I was sitting in my vehicle with the doors locked, so he couldn't get to me.

I looked into my rearview mirror to see if I was being followed. I wasn't sure about what this man was driving, but there was a big, hulking, black truck trying to ride my bumper.

"What can I do to get away from this guy?" I mumbled.

I knew it appeared that I talked to myself a lot, but I had to do that to keep myself focused. The fact that I was alone, always because of my missing children...I had no one to talk with, and I certainly didn't like that at all.

I had to focus on losing the big, hulking, black truck that was behind me. The truck was getting closer, and I could almost feel the driver breathing down my neck. I sped up, and he sped up. I changed lanes, and he changed lanes. He mimicked my every move. When he closed the distance between us, I could feel a gentle tap against my bumper. When that tap happened the first time, I was afraid the next bump would knock me off the road.

I knew I was headed in the direction of the county Sheriff's office. A couple more miles, and I could make a turn onto the parking lot. I would hopefully get some help.

The man sped up again, and I sped up, but I wasn't fast enough to get away from him. He banged into my bumper with an aggression that scared me. I drove faster, but he did, too.

Just a couple more minutes, and I could be at the Sheriff's office.

The man started to pass me, and I couldn't have that happen. He would be able to run me off the road, and I would crash into the deep ditch that would cause me great harm.

As he swerved toward me in his effort to get positioned at my side, I made a move toward him, and he moved over because my movement was so unexpected. It was a reflex action that caused him to run off the road into the deep ravine on the opposite side. I watched his big, hulking, black truck get swallowed up by the deep ravine.

I continued driving to the Sheriff's office to tell him about the vehicle that had driven off the road. A deputy was dispatched immediately to help the man in the big, hulking, black truck.

I did not leave the Sheriff's office because if the driver was still able to drive his truck, he would be after me again.

I waited around for what seemed forever until I saw the man from the truck enter the Sheriff's office in handcuffs. The Sheriff explained to me that this guy, Samuel Drake, had several warrants out for his arrest.

"Did he tell you why he was following me and trying to run me off the road?"

"I asked him, but he said he did nothing like that," said the Sheriff.

"He's lying," I said.

"Yes, ma'am."

"What are you going to do about the fact that he tried to kill me?" I asked angrily. "He probably was the man who did *this*." I gestured toward my shoulder.

"We're working on that and finding your children," the Sheriff said. "He probably knows where they are. We are questioning him about everything."

"What should I do? If I keep looking for my missing family and friend, his cohorts will come after me. I don't know how to get around town to go grocery shopping or to the doctor without being seen. You tell me what I should do."

"I'll have a deputy follow you home," the Sheriff said, trying to calm me. "If you have a garage, park your car inside. I will have my deputies patrol your street. The presence of patrol cars should keep them away from you."

"I hope so," I said. "Is that deputy available now?"

"Yes, I'll send Deputy Smith."

"Who?"

"Deputy Smith."

"No, not him. Do you have anyone else available?" I asked weakly.

"Not at the moment. Why not Deputy Smith?"

"Because of what happened the last time Deputy Smith was involved," I answered.

"I'll get him in here so you can tell us both what happened to make you not want his help," said the confused Sheriff.

Deputy Smith was called into the office, and when he appeared, I was so angry that my face was turning red as blood rushed into it.

"Why did you send that man after me? He said specifically that he was sent by Officer Smith."

"What are you talking about? What man?" sputtered the Deputy.

"That man who tried to kill me by running me off the road told me to meet him at the house."

"What house? What man?" he demanded.

"The man that is locked up back there," I said as I pointed to the double doors that read, *AUTHORIZED ONLY.*

"Who is locked up back there?" the Deputy asked the Sheriff.

"His ID said his name is Samuel Drake," the Sheriff replied.

86

Do you know him?"

"I don't know anyone named Samuel Drake."

"Go to the back and take a look at him," instructed the Sheriff.

The Deputy was gone for less than a minute, and then he told me that he did not know the man in custody.

"How did he know to use your name to get me to meet him at that house?" I asked the Deputy in a disbelieving tone.

"Where is this house?" the Sheriff asked.

"331 Valleyview."

"That house is unoccupied," said the Sheriff.

"That's what I figured," I said. "I didn't see anyone moving around. It really looked deserted to me. I still want to know how that guy knew to use your name, Deputy Smith?"

"I have no idea, Ms. Harris, but I intend to find out," the Deputy said in a huff. "I'll be back in a few minutes to follow you home. I want to have a talk with Samuel Drake."

Chapter 30

I waited for Deputy Smith to return. It seemed like forever, but when he walked through the door, he went over to the Sheriff and whispered in his ear. I could hear a word or two but not the whole whisper.

"What's going on?" I asked.

"I think we have located your missing children," explained the Sheriff. "You need to wait here. Deputy Smith and I will go check on their location." He then prepared to leave with Deputy Smith.

I stared at the two of them as they hurried out the door. I couldn't believe what they had told me. I sat and waited, waited, waited. When I could sit no longer, I paced, paced, paced. I glanced at the clock on the wall as the hands moved ever so slowly.

The throbbing in my shoulder was getting to me, so I sat down again. I was hoping that would ease the pain. The police radio in the other room was active and loud enough for me to pick up a word here and there.

"Shots fired!" was a phrase I heard, and I immediately became frightened, not for me, but for my children and Jed.

"What's happening?" I asked the dispatcher.

"I'm not sure, ma'am," whispered the dispatcher.

Another burst came across the radio: "We need back up!"

The dispatcher broadcasted to patrol deputies to respond to the location.

"What is going on!?" I demanded.

"Ma'am, I really don't know. I'll tell you as soon as they tell me."

"Are my kids there? Are they shooting at my kids?" I pleaded.

"I don't know," said the dispatcher.

Tears of fear and frustration came rushing out. I couldn't control them, so I left the room and proceeded to walk to the ladies room. I sat on the throne in the locked cubicle and cried until all of the tears stopped flowing.

I stood up, unlocked the door, and opened it...to see my three children and best friend standing there, waiting for me.

My mouth opened up wide, but nothing came out, no sounds of any kind. I couldn't believe what I was looking at in front of me.

"Mom, are you all right?" asked Emily.

When I heard her voice, I knew what I was seeing was real. The sound returned to my throat, and I screamed in tearful joy as I wrapped my good arm around my children.

Chapter 31

"Let's get out of here so you can tell me all about your excursion away from home," I said as I ushered my children out after the Sheriff took statements from each of them.

It was a short drive to the house but full of excitement on their parts and mine. I wanted so much just to hold each of my children and let them each know how much they were missed and loved. Of course, that included my friend, Jed. He was there for the kids, and I was glad they had him to hang onto for hope and help.

I picked up hamburgers and fries for all of us. Once we were finished with the food, I asked them to begin telling me everything.

"Emily, you were the first to disappear. Why did that happen?" I asked.

"Well—I was doing just what you said to do," Emily began. "I was watching the Greene house. Then, I felt someone walk up behind me. I thought it was Ryan or Ellen, so I didn't pay too much attention until the hand went over my mouth. Then, I knew I was in trouble."

"What happened next, Emily?"

"He pulled me off of the porch and told me not to make a sound. Then, he took me to the Greene house."

"What happened to you, Ryan?" I turned to my son.

Ryan swayed from side to side, wrinkled his nose, and finally spoke, "I really don't know. Something was placed over my face, and out I went."

"Did you get a look at that person?" I asked.

"No."

"You're up next, Ellen. What happened?"

"When you left me standing alone, I thought I saw someone I knew. As I moved closer to the person, he moved farther away from me. I was close to a car, someone opened the door, and it slammed into me, knocking the wind from me. I was shoved into the car and told not to make a sound."

"What was next?" I asked.

"He drove me to the Greene house, where I found Emily and Ryan," Ellen said. "We were all scared and afraid to talk."

"Did the man tell you why he was holding all of you? Did he say what he was going to do to you? Did he tell you anything at all?" I asked as I searched for answers.

"He said he was going to have to get rid of us because we could identify him," said Emily.

"Did any of you know this man?" I asked.

"No."

"No."

"No."

"When did Jed appear on the scene?" I continued with the questions.

"Someone hit me over the head when I was peeking into the window at the back of the Greene house," Jed spoke at last.

"Did you see the kids at that time?" I asked.

"No, but I knew they were in there."

"What happened after you were hit over the head?"

"I don't really know, but when I woke up, I was tied up and lying on the floor with the kids," Jed said. "They were tied up, too."

"Jed, did he tell you why he was planning to kill all of you and how he was going to do it?"

"Yes, he did. He was planning to shoot each of us and then burn the house down. He didn't want to leave any evidence."

"My loves, this is the best Christmas I could have," I said. "You are home, and I couldn't be happier." I motioned for them to come closer. I needed to hug them with one arm again.

"How did the police find you?" I continued.

"That was Emily's doing," said Jed. "She managed to stand up in front of a window. As soon as someone saw her with her mouth taped, they called the police."

"Is he the one who killed Otis Greene?" I asked.

"Yes, and it was a drug deal gone wrong."

"You know this isn't the end," I said. "There will be a trial, and you guys will have to relive it all over again."

Emily answered slowly, "We know, Mom, but we are glad this part is over, and we will always remember that SNOOPING CAN BE UN-MERRY."

ACKNOWLEDGMENTS

Janie C. Jessee, publisher of 12 of my books, must be acknowledged for allowing me to do what I must do—write.

A special thanks to Tammy Robinson Smith for asking me to start this little series.

ABOUT THE AUTHOR

Linda Hudson Hoagland of Tazewell, Virginia, a graduate of Southwest Virginia Community College, has won acclaim for many of her novels, including *Snooping Can Be Dangerous; Snooping Can Be Contagious; Snooping Can Be Devious; Snooping Can Be Doggone Deadly; Snooping Can Be Helpful–Sometimes; Snooping Can Be Uncomfortable; Snooping Can Be Scary; Snooping Can Be Regrettable; The Best Darn Secret; Onward & Upward;* and *Missing Sammy*—all published by Jan-Carol Publishing, Inc.

Other publications include *Dangerous Shadow, Crooked Road Stalker, Checking on the House, Death By Computer, The Backwards House, An Awfully Lonely Place, An Unjust Court,* five collections of short stories, and five collections of poetry.

Hoagland has written other fiction, nonfiction, poetry, and short stories that have been included in many anthologies, including *Broken Petals, Easter Lilies, Wild Daisies, Scattered Flowers, Daffodil Dreams, Snowy Trails, These Haunted Hills Books 1–6,* and several more.

Hoagland is a retired Tazewell County Schools System employee, where she worked as a purchase order clerk for almost 23 years. She is a proud mother of two sons.

COMING SOON

Lindsay Harris finds that her snooping has led her to the trial of the people who killed her neighbor, Otis Greene. All of them—Lindsay, Jed, Emily, Ellen, and Ryan—are asked to testify against the killers. There is no way of getting out of the trouble they may be subjected to in *Snooping Can Be a Trial*.

LINDSAY HARRIS
MURDER MYSTERY SERIES

BY LINDA HUDSON HOAGLAND

JAN-CAROL PUBLISHING, INC.

Linda Hudson Hoagland has authored and published many books, including poetry, and is an accomplished writer. She has received recognition and numerous awards throughout her writing career.

WWW.LINDASBOOKSANDANGELS.COM

97